SO-AHD-663

BRIDES, MIDWIVES, AND WIDOWS

S E T T L I N G   T H E   W E S T

BRIDES, MIDWIVES, AND WIDOWS

JUDITH BENTLEY

TWENTY–FIRST CENTURY BOOKS

A Division of Henry Holt and Company
New York

Twenty-First Century Books
A Division of Henry Holt and Company, Inc.
115 West 18th Street
New York, NY 10011

Henry Holt® and colophon are trademarks of
Henry Holt and Company, Inc.
Publishers since 1866

Library of Congress Cataloging-in-Publication Data
Bentley, Judith.
Brides, midwives, and widows / Judith Bentley. — 1st ed.
p. cm. — (Settling the West)
Includes bibliographical references (p.) and index.
1. Women pioneers—West (U.S.)—History—Juvenile literature.
2. West (U.S.)—Social life and customs—Juvenile literature.
I. Title. II. Series.

F596.B38 1995	94–39897
978′.0082—dc20	CIP
	AC

ISBN 0-8050-2994-X
First Edition 1995

Cover design by Kelly Soong
Interior design by Helene Berinsky

Photo Credits
pp. 2, 50, 65, 73: North Wind Picture Archives; pp. 13, 17, 28, 82: The Bettmann
Archive; p. 18: Oregon Historical Society/OrHi 56364. Drawing by Joseph Drayton;
pp. 20, 77: Nevada Historical Society; p. 22: Oregon Historical Society/OrHi 21681; p.
23: Oregon Historical Society/OrHi 260; pp. 31, 40: Museum of History and Industry;
p. 34: Oregon Historical Society/CN 017573; p. 37: Oregon Historical Society/OrHi
61318; p. 43: UPI/Bettmann; p. 45: Puget Sound Maritime Historical Society; p. 53:
Gown from the collection of the Museum of History and Industry, Seattle, Washington
(1967.4264.1). Photograph by Julie Lassiter; p. 56: Harry T. Peters Collection/The New
York Historical Society; p. 68: Oregon Historical Society/OrHi 3; p. 79: Oregon
Historical Society/CN 022599.

EDITOR'S NOTE

A great deal of research went into finding interesting first-person accounts that would give the reader a vivid picture of life on the western frontier. In order to retain the "flavor" of these accounts, original spelling and punctuation have been kept in most instances.

History told in the words of men and women who lived at the time lets us become a part of their lives . . . lives of ordinary people who met extraordinary challenges to settle the West.

—P.C.

ACKNOWLEDGMENTS

I'd like to acknowledge the help of the following people in providing resources or undertaking the mundane but important work of research and permission gathering: Laura Phipps, Anne Bentley, Nancy Valaas, Virginia Phipps, Jeanne Macdonald, and Esther Mumford.

—J.B.

CONTENTS

Introduction 11

1 The First Women 17

2 The Invisible Women 26

3 Marriages of Convenience 33

4 Love and Marriage 48

5 Midwives 55

6 Neighbors 64

7 Women on Their Own 72

Source Notes 84

Further Reading 90

Index 94

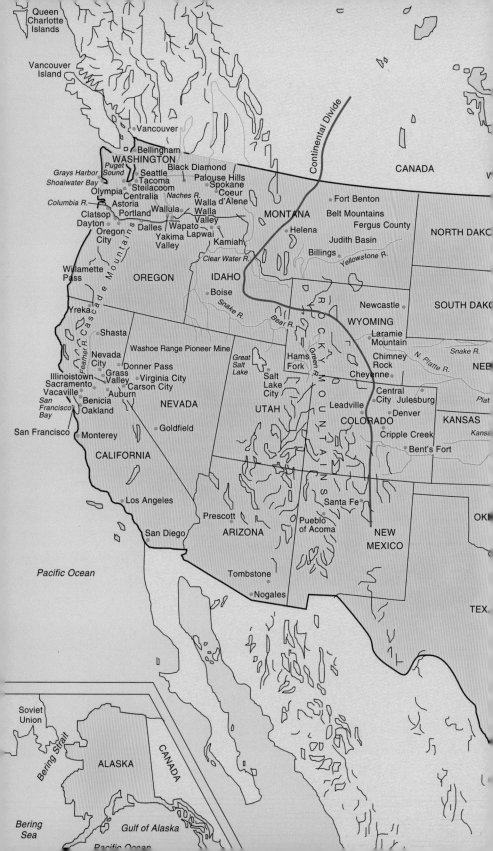

MAJOR TRAILS TO THE WEST

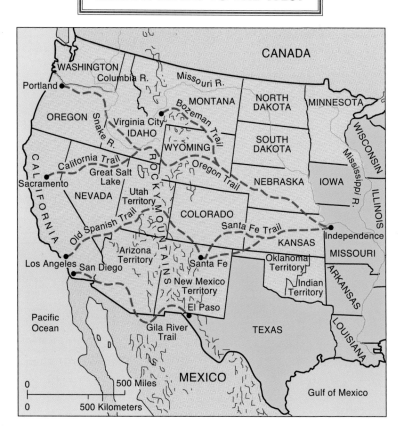

INTRODUCTION

In the first 100 years of exploration and settlement of the Far West, women were scarce. Explorers left their wives at home, if they had them. Priests and monks came before nuns. Fur trappers were loners or had Native American wives. Miners were usually men. Even when the great pioneer migrations of the late 1840s began, only one in ten emigrants was a woman.[1]

"Bring as many girls as you can," Narcissa Whitman wrote back to her sister in New York State, urging her to come west in 1846, "but let every young man bring a wife, for he will want one after he gets here, if he never did before."[2]

Because women were so rare in San Francisco, they were treated like queens. When they walked on the streets in 1849, the men stared. "Doorways filled instantly, and little islands in the streets were thronged with men who seemed to gather in a moment, and who remained immovable till the spectacle passed from their incredulous gaze."[3]

"We were all in the habit of running to our cabin doors in Denver, on the arrival of a lady, to gaze at her as earnestly as at any other rare natural curiosity," said a miner in Colorado in 1860.[4]

Even twenty years later, Caroline Leighton felt like an oddity among miners in California. "I am afraid I should have had a very mistaken impression of my importance if I had lived long among them. At every stoppingplace they made little fires in their frying pans, and set them around me, to keep off the mosquitoes, while I took my meal. As the columns of smoke rose about me I felt like a heathen goddess, to whom incense was being offered."[5]

In dances, men often had to tie handkerchiefs around their arms to designate themselves as females. In a dance of sixty-five people, there might be three real women.

"Would give my little finger to go to the theater or museum with some certain Baltimore girls, tonight—hush memory—or I'll go mad," wrote a male gold seeker.[6]

It was not just the company of women at dances or theaters that the men missed, but their very practical value. The sentiment of the miners "was somewhat intensified by the extreme difficulty they found in doing women's work," Leighton observed. "One of them, now an eminent physician, pricked and scarred his fingers in the most distressing manner, in attempting to sew on his buttons, and patch the rents in his garments."[7]

When Elkanah Walker's wife had been gone from their mission in Oregon Territory for a time, he wrote her a letter telling why he missed her: "I am tired of keeping an old bachelor's hall. Things do not go to suit me when I come in from work tired almost to death. I want someone to get me a good supper & let me take my ease & when I

There were few women in the West of the 1800s. Those who went west to become brides often faced years of hard frontier life.

am very tired in the morning I want someone to get up & get breakfast & let me lay in bed & take my rest. More than all I want my wife where I can have her company & to cheer me up when the blue devils chain me down. . . ."[8]

Women were also valued because it was thought they had a civilizing effect. "We find we are to enjoy at last, what we have so much needed, the sweet, the gentle, the saving influence of women," wrote John McCracken, a San Francisco lawyer, in a letter to his sister.[9]

The problem was not that women were stay-at-homes, too timid to go west. Rather, a woman could not easily travel alone. Many emigration companies that booked passages on ships to the West Coast would take only men.

Consider the plight of Sophia Eastman, who wanted to go to California as a teacher in the gold rush year of 1849. "A woman who dare go to California, virtually avows that she is not afraid of men," cautioned her Aunt Harriet. "Tell her to meet them as fellow beings—not merely as masculine bipeds. . . . And tell her to engrave on her heart's core that all men, even vicious and depraved men, always respect a true woman, who respects herself."[10]

Sophia did go west, but she never found a teaching job. Her only offer was from a school that closed during the rainy season. In the meantime she supported herself as a nurse in a hospital but had trouble collecting her wages. Despite her firm intentions to be independent, after several proposals she finally married one man who had been the most persistent and faithful.

Even women who were looking for husbands found it indelicate to come without some pretense of work. That was not a problem, however, for the young daughters in families who emigrated. "There is a great many young men loves me about Hear," wrote sixteen-year-old Rachel Malick to her married sister back in Illinois.[11]

The shortage of women prompted ingenious solutions. The first European-American men to come west—fur trappers for the Hudson's Bay Company, French-Canadian voyageurs, the Rocky Mountain men—found Native American wives. Some men who decided to stay eventually brought their wives from home. Others used advertisements, letters home, and far-fetched schemes to bring women they had never met to become their brides.

For women, such long-distance arrangements were a gamble. Only the most adventuresome undertook the journey. Far from parents and friends, the transplanted brides found few neighbors to share the hardships and no doctors and few midwives to assist at births. Many brides went to work immediately on their husbands' farms or in laundries; some soon became widows who had to support children on their own.

Yet, in addition to raising children and hard manual labor, the first women were also expected to civilize the rough frontier: to start churches and schools, take care of their neighbors, and establish the ties that made a community. As they did, they kept diaries and wrote long letters back "home."

On the rolling decks of ships sailing around Cape Horn, by wavering campfires at the end of a day on the trails, finally inside crude cabins or tents on lonely nights, the women recorded the large and small dramas of their lives. In their words, this book tells their story: how girls became hopeful young brides, hardworking wives and mothers, neighbors, midwives, and widows—all forged by the West into a new American woman.

THE FIRST WOMEN

When European and American men encountered Native Americans in the West, women provided an important link between the two cultures. From Sacagawea, a translator for Lewis and Clark, to Julia Rivet, the enterprising wife of fur trader Peter Skene Ogden, Native American women more easily crossed racial lines. With no white women for a thousand miles, Salish women at Spokane House, a fur trading post, put on European clothes to give ballroom dancing a whirl.

Sacagawea was a Shoshone Indian woman who served as an interpreter for the Lewis and Clark expedition in 1804–1805.

Many of the first marriages between the newcomers and Native American women were for economic reasons. The native women had relatives who trapped and traded furs. Daniel Williams Harmon, who was working for the North West Company in Canada, described the first marriage proposal he received in 1802. A Cree chief "wished to have his Daughter with the white people and he almost persuaded me to accept of her, for I was sure that while I had the Daughter I should not only have the Fathers hunts but those of his relations also."[1]

Besides the trading advantage they brought, Native American women knew how to live in the wilderness. Jason Lee, an early missionary to the Oregon Territory, envied the French Canadians who had come with the fur trappers and settled with Native American wives: "Very

Native American women married to white trappers played an important part in fur trading.

fortunate indeed are these happy-go-lucky voyageurs in finding such capable women to make them homes."[2] The wife Lee brought with him from the East died young, as did the second wife he then married.

Native American women knew where passes led through the mountains, where rapids clogged the rivers, or when trouble was afoot. If those reasons weren't enough, there was pure physical attraction. "She was the most beautiful Indian woman I ever saw," wrote Joe Meek of his wife, Mountain Lamb, "and when she was mounted on her dapple gray horse, which cost me three hundred dollars, she made a fine show. She wore a skirt of beautiful blue broadcloth, and a bodice and leggins of scarlet cloth, of the very finest make. Her hair was braided and fell over her shoulders, a scarlet silk handkerchief, tied on hood fashion, covered her head; and the finest embroidered moccasins her feet."[3]

Indian girls did not become brides until they had "come to womanhood"—their first menstrual period. This event was marked among the Paiute of northern Nevada by a twenty-five-day ritual. "The young woman is set apart under the care of two of her friends, somewhat older, and a little wigwam, called a teepee, just big enough for the three, is made for them, to which they retire," reported Sarah Winnemucca.

Then she went through strengthening labors. "Every day, three times a day, she must gather and pile up as high as she can, five stacks of wood. . . . At the end of twenty-five days she returns to the family lodge. . . . It is thus publicly known that there is another marriageable woman, and any young man interested in her, or wishing to form an alliance, comes forward."[4]

A Paiute couple in native dress

Among the Paiute, an interested male would not speak to the young woman or visit her family but would attempt to attract her attention by showing his horsemanship or some other skill. The courtship might go on for a year until she made up her mind.

Julia Rivet was the Indian stepdaughter of a French-Canadian fur trapper and already a widow when she came to the attention of Peter Skene Ogden, a Canadian fur trader working for the Hudson's Bay Company. To woo her, Ogden called on her many times. To marry her, he brought a herd of fifty horses, including a spirited gold-colored mare with creamy mane and tail. One by one he had the horses led to her mother's lodge, where they were accepted, but there was no sign of Julia. Finally he sent the golden mare. The stillness was broken by many cries, and in a flash of color, Julia came riding out on the golden mare in white buckskin and beadwork, her face showing acceptance.[5]

Most Native American women who entered mixed-race marriages had far less choice. "The man is thought a decent wooer who comes with money in his pocket to an Indian lodge," wrote William H. Dixon.[6] He said an Indian girl could be bought for $20 or for a cup of sugar or, more expensively, for fifteen guns and fifteen blankets.

These early marriages were usually made "according to the custom of the day," which meant there was no minister or priest present, no marriage license, and no written record. If there was a ceremony, it combined European-American and Indian customs, which varied from tribe to tribe.

At Fort Astoria on the Columbia River, a marriage was arranged to keep the peace and trading relations with the Cowlitz Indians. Chief How How brought his daughter down the river by canoe to marry a young gentleman at the fort. The chief received presents of blankets, guns, hardware, and tobacco. There were speeches of friendship and a banquet of roast pork, elk, salmon, swan, and rum, followed by toasts and dancing to bagpipes and fiddles.[7]

Fort Astoria in 1813

Some of the marriages lasted a lifetime and were made official when priests and ministers arrived in the territories. But gradually, as large numbers of Indians died from disease and as settlers came to the West, a stigma was attached to someone with an Indian wife. Men who married Indian women were called "squaw men" by people who did not intend it as a compliment. When an Anglican clergyman came to Fort Vancouver in 1836, he said the chief factor (business agent), John McLoughlin, was "living in sin" because he had a Native American wife.[8]

What did the Native American women think of these

marriages? Their actions show they did not give up Indian ways. The wife of James Birnie took off from Astoria once a year in a large canoe to go to Shoalwater Bay for elk hunting, clamming, and cranberry picking with her people. Angus McDonald's wife, Catherine, could not live more than half the year in their house at Old Fort Colville. As a twelve-year-old she had accompanied her father, who was half Mohawk and half French or Scotch, on fur trapping expeditions with white men, at one time reaching the Pacific Ocean. No wonder such a girl "could not be much indoors" when she grew up. Instead, Catherine spent half of each year with her *tilicums*, or relatives and friends.

When Caroline Leighton visited Old Fort Colville, she found that Catherine's oldest daughter, Christine, kept house for her father. But she, too, did not like to be confined. "I asked her where she liked best to be, and she said, with the Blackfeet Indians because they had the prettiest dances, and could do such beautiful bead-work; and

Marguerite McLoughlin was the Native American wife of John McLoughlin, chief factor at Fort Vancouver. They lived at the fort from 1825 to 1846.

described their working on the softened skins of elk, deer, and antelope, making dresses for chiefs and warriors."[9]

The children of these marriages were called half-breeds or the French word *métis*. Many of the daughters married mountain men, American fur trappers; but the sons could not cross racial boundaries so easily. The choices they made between Indian and European-American life were difficult. At great expense, John McLoughlin sent two of his half-breed sons to England for their education, but the third he kept "a common Indian."

"I daresay the heathen is the happiest of them," wrote Letitia Hargrave in 1840, "as the father is constantly upbraiding the others with the ransom they have cost him."[10]

Many remained proud of their heritage. "It is true that our savage origin is humble, but it is meet that we honor our mothers as well as our fathers," wrote one méti. "Why should we concern ourselves about what degree of mixture we possess of European or Indian blood? If we have ever so little of either gratitude or filial love, should we not be proud to say, 'We are Metis!'?"[11]

Mourning Dove, the daughter of an Indian woman and a half-breed father, was born in a canoe on the Kootenai River in Idaho during the mining rush of 1888. As an adult she began carrying a typewriter around with her because she thought that the Native American oral tradition might be lost. She used the typewriter to write down the sacred legends the eldest Indians told her.

"I found a rich field that had hardly been touched by the hand of the white man, although he has attempted it several times. But a white man cannot understand what an Indian will see, and cannot know that which comes from the heart and not only from the voice. . . . I will feel well rewarded if I have preserved for the future generations the folklore of my ancestors."[12]

Half in one culture and half in another, this generation became not just translators of the language to the new people rushing westward, but preservers and interpreters of one culture to another.

2

THE INVISIBLE WOMEN

Long before Narcissa Whitman and Eliza Spalding were the "first white women to cross the Rockies" came a few lone women in the category of "adventuress." Such a woman was Jane Barnes, who was tending bar in Portsmouth, England, in 1812 when Donald McTavish made her a proposal. McTavish was on his way to the North West Company's fur trading post at Fort George on the Columbia River. He promised to buy Barnes all the fancy dresses and hats she wanted and a pension afterward, if she would go with him. He didn't promise her marriage.

Barnes accepted McTavish's offer and became the first white woman in the Pacific Northwest. Arriving with her hats and dresses, she passed from McTavish's favor to that of another trader at the fort, Alexander Henry. When both gentlemen drowned, she sailed for Canton, China, with a willing skipper.[1] Jane Barnes was not a woman who liked to stay home.

Although Barnes's name has survived, most of the women who came to the Far West unmarried were recorded only as numbers and curiosities. The discovery of gold in California in 1849 brought some of those numbers. Most came, knowingly or unknowingly, as prostitutes. Some 5,000 Chilean women were reported in San Francisco in the first six months. Hundreds of Mexican women from San Blas and Mazatlán came in an indenture arrangement. They had to work for a certain number of years in fandango houses, the poor man's brothels, to earn their freedom.

In May 1850, the newspaper *Alta California* reported the arrival of another boatload of women: "ENLARGEMENT OF SOCIETY—We are pleased to notice by the arrival from sea Saturday, the appearance of some fifty or sixty of the fairer sex in full bloom. They are from all quarters—some from Yankeeland, others from John Bull country [England], and quite a constellation from merry France. One Frenchman brings twenty—all, they say, beautiful! The bay was dotted by flotillas of young men, on the announcement of this extraordinary importation."[2]

Besides these statistics and the gleeful reports of their countries of origin, almost nothing is known or recorded of these women who were imported by men.

For a few, life in the mining camps was an opportunity. The sight of a piano being carted across the mountains was a sign that a "hurdy-gurdy" house would soon be open in the camps. Hurdy-gurdies were primitive stringed instruments turned by a crank. The more sophisticated parlor would have piano playing in the downstairs room with "hurdy-gurdy" girls who charged a dollar for a waltz. Half of that dollar went to the management, in part to pay the piano player and in part for carting the piano.

Merely the sight of women in plumes, feathers, silks, and lace stockings offered a spot of gaiety in the hard life of

Hurdy-gurdy girls brought entertainment to camps in the early West.

the miners. In saloons and gambling houses, men paid women to sit with them near the bar or at a card table. A very few women became wealthy, like Julia Bulette, who arrived in Virginia City, Nevada, soon after the discovery of silver.

Most, however, had little choice in coming and little alternative when they arrived. In Canton, China, where people were starving and women had little or no value, it was common practice to sell daughters into slavery. Chinese organizations in San Francisco imported such "daughters of joy."

"I was nineteen when this man came to my mother and said that in America there was a great deal of gold," Wong Ah So recounted. "Even if I just peeled potatoes there, he told my mother I would earn seven or eight dollars a day, and if I was willing to do any work at all I would earn lots of money. He was a laundryman, but said he earned plenty of money. He was very nice to me, and my mother liked him, so my mother was glad to have me go with him as his wife. I thought that I was his wife, and was very grateful that he was taking me to such a grand, free country, where everyone was rich and happy."

Two weeks after she arrived in San Francisco, Wong Ah So learned she had been brought as a slave and would be forced to work as a prostitute. "When we first landed in San Francisco we lived in a hotel in Chinatown, a nice place, but one day . . . a woman came to see me. She was young, very pretty, and all dressed in silk. She told me that I was not really Huey Yow's wife, but she had asked him to buy her a slave, that I belonged to her, and must go with her, but she would treat me well, and I could buy back my freedom, if I was willing to please, and be agreeable. . . ."

Wong Ah So did not believe her, but Huey Yow told her it was true, "that he was not my husband, he did not care about me, and that this was something that happened all the time."[3] Seven months later Wong Ah So was rescued from her slavery by a San Francisco mission.

Later, when Japanese immigration replaced Chinese, Japanese girls and women, too, were brought as prostitutes to Denver's red-light district in the 1860s and to Portland and Seattle. Sailboats owned by Northwest sawmills would ship lumber to various parts of the world and return with Japanese women.

"At the ports of Victoria, Vancouver, Bellingham, Olympia and elsewhere, there were no immigration offices, so the girls were unloaded at night. There was a boss also on the American side who took the girls at some hundred dollars each and sold them to local bosses," said Bunshiro Tazuma, who worked as a cook. "Oppressed by a boss, it is said they could do nothing but weep for four or five years."[4]

The men's lives were little better. Asian men were not allowed to bring wives with them at first. "The price of a prostitute was unexpectedly high, while the wage for a Japanese railroad worker was only a dollar a day for working twelve hours. Those laborers lived in wretched barracks like pigpens, on meals such as dumpling soup and the like."[5]

In such a life, a woman could be an object of wonder. One young Chinese woman was the bride of "Old" Wing Kee in a remote mining camp. "We used to watch her comb her hair in the mornings. Old Kee said we could, if we never got smart, or tried to sass her, or made any noise. She'd take her long black hair and smooth it out over her ear—just like a bird's wing. . . . It was neat as a pin and yet somehow, I dunno, it wasn't plain, it was fancy, or it seemed fancy. She wore silk trousers and an embroidered jacket and she had the tiniest feet you ever saw—tiny as a baby's. Her hands were tiny too, and white, with little

Chen Chong was the first Chinese merchant in Seattle. This 1866 picture shows him and his bride in clothes borrowed for their wedding. His wife was kidnapped and sold into slavery. He found her in Honolulu some years later.

fingers, and they folded in sort of, like a bird's claw, only not bony."[6]

Little do we know what she thought of the attention. Nor did Jane Barnes, the Mexican indentured servant, the hurdy-gurdy girl, or the prostitute leave diaries and journals. Only when married, educated women arrived did the written record of ordinary brides and wives begin.

MARRIAGES OF CONVENIENCE

Are females wanted?" Narcissa Prentiss asked Dr. Samuel Parker when he came through New York State seeking missionaries to the tribes of the Far West. He, in turn, asked the American Board of Missions.[1]

Yes, females were wanted, came the answer. But not alone, not single, not unmarried.

By the 1830s, Native American wives were common in the West, and a few enterprising "adventuresses" had made places for themselves, but most women could not go west alone. It was dangerous, it was expensive, it did not seem right. The American Board of Missions informed Narcissa that no matter how good her intentions, she would have to marry.

Thus began many marriages of convenience, marriages for reasons other than pure romance. Wives were needed, and so were husbands if a woman wanted to pursue her dreams.

In a situation similar to Narcissa Prentiss's was Mary

Richardson, who gave up a man she wanted to marry because he was not religious. Instead she accepted the marriage proposal of Elkanah Walker, and in 1838 they set out on the long horseback journey west to bring Christianity to the Indians.

The marriage matched both of their vocations, but it did not seem to make either one happy at first.

"I am almost in despair and without hope of his ever being pleased or satisfied with [me]," Mary wrote in her journal. "I do not know what course to pursue. I can never, with all my care, make myself what he would like me to be."[2]

Indeed, she was ill at ease with her new identity, as she wrote back in her first letter home. "Nothing gives me

Mary Richardson Walker

such a solitery feeling as to be called Mrs. Walker. It would sound so sweet to have someone now and then call me Mary or by mistake say Miss Richardson. But that one expression, Mrs. W., seems at once to indicate a change unlike all other changes. My father, my mother, my brothers, my sisters, all answer to the name Richardson. The name W. seems to me to imply a severed branch. Such I feel to be. . . ."[3]

Hard as the first months were—traveling by horseback, sidesaddle, thousands of miles, Mary pregnant much of the way, sharing tents with other couples—eventually the Walkers had a happy marriage, enough that Elkanah could write how much he missed her (and her cooking) when she was away.

Missionary wives were some of the first white women to reach the western wilderness, and their arrival caused change. When they stayed at Fort Vancouver, the Hudson's Bay Company's post, Narcissa Prentiss Whitman and Eliza Spalding ate meals with the men instead of separately, as the Indian wives had done. "When the missionary ladies came it was quite different," wrote the half-Indian daughter of John McLoughlin at the fort. "Then we mingled more."[4]

One national law, however, caused more than a change in dining habits. In 1850, the United States government actually put a dollar value on wives. Under the Donation Land Claim Act, land was available to couples who would farm it—320 acres to a single man and 320 more if he was married. "I had my first offer of marriage when I was 13, and from then till I was 24 I had numerous proposals," wrote Jennie Stevenson Miller in her journal. "But I had a pretty strong suspicion that many of the men who wanted to marry me wanted the extra land they could get if they were married."[5] She did not intend to become merely a "donation claim bride."

Despite this giveaway and the great pioneer migrations of the 1840s and 1850s, women were still outnumbered in the Wild West. "To supply the bachelors of the West with wives, to furnish the pining maidens of the East with husbands, and to better equalize the present disposition of the sexes in these two sections of our country, has been one of the difficulties of the age," a Missouri newspaper proclaimed.[6]

Eliza Farnham, a New York prison matron, decided to help out. When her husband died in San Francisco in 1848, she had to go there to settle his estate and advertised for a company of prospective brides to go with her. She wanted only "intelligent, virtuous and efficient women over age twenty-five," she said, and she required testimonials from clergymen or town officials concerning the women's education and character.

Mrs. Farnham believed that the presence of women "would be one of the surest checks upon many of the evils that are apprehended there."[7]

"Went to church 3 times today," wrote one California miner who probably did not see himself as one of the evils. "A few ladies present, does my eyes good to see a woman once more. Hope Mrs. Farnham will bring 10,000."[8]

Unfortunately for the miner, she didn't. Mrs. Farnham became ill while planning the venture and only two women came with her.

If white women were in short supply, black women were even more scarce. "There are quite a number of colored men in this county who are living in single blessed-

Louisa Thacker Flowers was born in Boston. She and her husband, Alvin, came to Oregon in the 1860s.

ness," wrote Horace Cayton, publisher of a black newspaper in Seattle. They "would willingly change their way of living were there sufficient damsels of their own race to choose from," he lamented.[9]

In the Arizona mining camps, black wives tried to find brides for the single, boisterous men in the camps. Letters were sent back east promising suitable females a free trip, a secure marriage to an upstanding worker, and a good home.

When these mail-order brides arrived, however, they did not always find a young husband. The older miners demanded first choice. Their wives had died from repeated childbirths under unsanitary conditions, and their children needed new mothers.

In Colorado, too, "some of the cowboys, who had lived alone until they were on the verge of being old bachelors, advertised for a wife," recounted Attie Long Thompson. "Women came from as far east as Pennsylvania to marry these men, who would send them money to come on." Disappointed women didn't have to stay. "Some of the women took just one look at the men and then caught the first train back home, providing they had the money to do this," Attie continued.[10]

Over the years, the female shortage lessened, but the Civil War increased the imbalance. The New England states alone had 30,000 unattached women, some widows of Civil War soldiers or just women in towns where all the men had died in the same battle. In mill towns like Lowell, Massachusetts, many mills had closed, leaving women unemployed.

The Puget Sound country, in contrast, was a region where men outnumbered women nine to one. In 1860, the *Puget Sound Herald* of Steilacoom advertised an open meeting for bachelors to discuss the problem of the shortage of women.

Shortly thereafter, twenty-two-year-old Asa Shinn Mercer arrived in the territory, freshly graduated from Franklin College in Ohio. Mercer wanted to start a university, but he could find few students. He came up with an alternative scheme. He would go east, he told the legislature and bachelors in the community, and recruit women as teachers, seamstresses, and milliners.

Despite his good intentions, Mercer could persuade only nine women, ages fifteen to twenty-five, to return with him in 1864. Eight of these "Mercer Girls" married within the first year. The ninth, Lizzie Ordway, had never intended to "relinquish the advantages of single blessedness."[11] Instead she truly became a teacher and then a school superintendent.

Undaunted and still unmarried, Mercer went east again two years later, promising women who would come back with him jobs worth at least four dollars a week in gold. One newspaper accused him, instead, of "seeking to carry off young girls for the benefit of miserable old bachelors."

The newspaper also criticized any woman who booked passage. "It may well be doubted whether any girl who goes to seek a husband is worthy to be a decent man's wife, or is ever likely to be."[12] Because of delays in finding a ship and the bad publicity, Mercer recruited only one hundred passengers, including families, widows, orphans, a few single men, and thirty-six unmarried women.

Those on board, however, were delighted with the adventure. "The steamer, with a lessened quota of passengers, left New York January 6, 1866, and ran at once into a storm, which lasted two days," wrote Harriet F. Stevens. "As we recovered our normal condition we began to look about us. With great satisfaction we found that we had a party of intelligent, amiable, sprightly people."

Miss Stevens decided that the women who shared her willingness to come west probably had more than mere marriage in mind: "The unmarried ladies are mostly from New England, and can boast a fair share of beauty and culture, which characterize the best society of that region. It is impossible that the lovely girls who are with us should have left the East because their chances of matrimony were hopeless. . . . Their bright faces, wit and sound sense are . . . such that they cannot fail to be desirable members of society in a new country."[13]

Sailing through the Strait of Magellan, Mercer almost lost some of his passengers at Lota, Chile, where Spaniards offered the women jobs if they would stay. Finally, the steamship *Continental* arrived in San Francisco on April 24, 1866, where its arrival caused quite a stir.

There was much rejoicing when the steamer Continental *brought a group of women to the West in 1866.*

"As we neared the dock . . . we could see the wharves completely lined with men anxious, no doubt, to obtain a view of the party . . . ," wrote Ann S. Conner, who was on board. "Great numbers came off to the steamer in boats, and offered large sums of money for the privilege of coming onboard; but the Captain declined their offers."[14]

Twenty of the women decided to stay in San Francisco. The rest went on to Seattle in a lumber schooner, the *Tanner*. "All the men in Seattle that could get suits did so, and others got new overalls and were on the dock when the *Tanner* arrived," wrote Roger Conant, a journalist who came along on the voyage.[15]

Within a few weeks, most of the women had married. "This morning an old back woodsman who could neither read or write, visited Seattle to inspect the party, and see if he could not secure a wife," wrote Conant. "He was introduced about 3 this afternoon to widow W. who brought out with her a Mother and three interesting sons, the neck of the youngest of whom we were on the point of wringing at least a dozen times during the voyage. At six he offered her his heart and hand; was accepted and at 9 o'clock, just one hour ago they were married."[16]

There was disappointment, too, for some of the men who had expected wives among the Mercer Girls. One man had given Mercer $300 to contact and bring back a young lady his friends had found for him in Ohio. Mercer never contacted the woman but instead brought someone else with, ironically, the same name.

"I'm the feller what sent $300 by Mercer to bring you out for my wife," the young farmer introduced himself to the lady he thought was his bride. "I suppose you are as willin' to get married this arternoon as any other time as I must be ter home by sundown to milk the cows and feed the pigs," he proposed.[17] When he discovered the woman was not his intended, he went home a sad man.

Others were luckier. Asa Mercer married Annie E. Stevens in July. Ida May Barlow married Albert Smith Pinkham in the Occidental Hotel. "That evening all the young people in town came down to the hotel and made merry to the strains of the Seattle Band," Ida May wrote, "and the Indians lined up outside the door and looked curiously in at the people and wondered at all the strange white people who made so much ado about a mere squaw."[18]

Despite Mercer's valiant attempts, the gender imbalance continued. It was even worse for men from other countries. Signe Ashland describes how she came to America as a very young bride from Sweden. "In 1910 I came by myself from Sundsvall in northern Sweden when I was just fifteen years old. Gunnar was cousin to all of us, and when he was home to Sweden one day I was cooking and washing the dishes and Gunnar tapped my dad on the shoulder. He said, 'This is the one I want. Don't give her away.'

"So later when he sent for me I went to Sundsvall to buy clothes and a ticket. And then, oh my, I was on the way to heaven!"[19]

Japanese men, too, decided they must have wives if they were ever to be happy in the United States. Although they came thirty to forty years later, Japanese "picture brides" knew little more of their husbands than the Mercer Girls. Arranged marriages were normal in Japan. "In my girlhood days it was out of the question for marry for love freely," recounts Hideyo Yokoyama. "It was the way of

Japanese women to marry a husband chosen by her parents. As the saying goes, 'Past, present and future—there is no free place for women.'"[20]

So it was not unnatural that Japanese men abroad found wives by writing home to relatives and exchanging pictures with prospective brides. Women who married on paper before even meeting their husbands were called "picture brides."

"I am one who made a photo marriage . . . ," wrote Tsuruyo Akiba Takami. She was married by registration in

Japanese picture brides in California around 1920

August 1915 to a man who was running a laundry in Washington State. "I left Japan dressed in pure Japanese style—kimono with light blue background designed with white waves and a plover flying. I had on a Hakata sash—white striped with black, blue and orange—and Japanese sandals with orange straps."

Tsuruyo knew she would need strength to leave her homeland forever. "On the way from Kobe to Yokohama I looked at Mt. Fuji standing loftily against the cloudless blue sky and in that moment I resolved: A woman going to America, depending on a husband she has never seen, should have the noble spirit of this majestic mountain."

Her husband had warned her about the hard life of an immigrant, which she discovered soon enough. When she landed in Seattle in 1918, at the age of twenty-three, Tsuruyo was held in the immigration office for two weeks to be inspected for trachoma, an eye infection. Her husband came to see her from Spokane, nearly 300 miles away, but had to return without her.

"I was kept for fourteen long days. On the first morning for breakfast I was served oatmeal. In Japan oats is food for poor people. At the idea that in America they had only oats to eat, my eyes filled with tears."[21]

When she was finally released from immigration, Tsuruyo traveled to Spokane by herself "without knowing the geography of the place or the language." She arrived at night at her husband's house and then had to get up at six the next morning to work.

"My husband was running the Rainier Laundry, with two other people . . . doing washing, ironing and pick-up-and-delivery service. Each man had charge of one of the three jobs. At noon I had to prepare a meal for twelve. The

A Japanese immigrant often established a laundry service and needed a hardworking picture bride to help with the business.

employees worked from 8 A.M. to 5 P.M., but I began to fix the dinner at 5 P.M., cooking for 5 or 6 persons, and then after that I started my night work. The difficult ironing and pressing was left for me. At that time ladies' blouses were high-necked and long-sleeved, with much silk lace and other decoration. I could barely iron two blouses an hour, taking great pains to press out each scallop with the point of the iron. Frequently I had to work till twelve or one o'clock."

Only on Saturday did the laundry close early so the family could do their grocery shopping. "On Saturday evenings we went to movies or shows. On Sundays we went to ball games and such, but we didn't have any vacations."[22]

Teiko Matsui Tomita came to Wapato, Washington, in 1921 and remained there for the next sixty years. Separated from her parents, five miles from the nearest neighbor, and usually alone with her children, Teiko wrote "tanka," a thirty-one-syllable form of Japanese poetry. Her last verse preserves the hopeful attitude of a bride:

> "Live happily,"
> Said my parents
> Holding my hands.
> Their touch
> Even now in my hands
>
> Yakima Valley
> The spring storm raging
> Even in the house
> A cloud of sand
> Sifts in
>
> As we busily pick beans
> Even the breeze stirring
> The weeds at our feet
> Feels hot

"Soon the heat will be gone"
While picking beans
I encourage my children
And myself

Carefully grafting
Young cherry trees
I believe in the certainty
They will bud
In the coming spring[23]

4

LOVE AND MARRIAGE

Mail-order marriages began in mystery, but in more conventional marriages the bride and groom had known each other, some for years, some for a month.

"Boone Johnson was a neighbor. He was 19 and a likely lad," recounts a woman known only as Mrs. Boone Johnson. "I was nearly 16, and Boone and I had been going together some." When he got a job driving a wagon west, "I didn't like him going clear out to Oregon and me staying, for I was afraid we would never see each other again. We decided to get married, but my father absolutely refused permission. He said we were both too young."

Young she was, but love and Oregon fever were stronger. "My married sister and one of my brothers had joined the wagon train, so I didn't say anything to my folks, but when the train pulled out I joined it." The young couple were married once they crossed the Missouri River, out of reach of United States law. While Boone drove the wagon, his bride did the cooking to pay her way. Eventually they settled in Oregon and had eleven children.[1]

Once in the West, girls who had come with their families had no trouble finding husbands. The shortage of women meant they were often married before they were really women.

In the spring of 1855, at the age of fourteen, Elizabeth Shepard traveled with her father down the Columbia River to Portland to buy some fruit trees. Because the river was rough, their travel was slow, and they spent the night in the cabin of a man named John Dodd.

"When he found out I was upwards of 14 years old, he said he had a friend named Henry Holtgrieve, who was looking for a wife. He asked Father when we would be back. He said he would arrange to have his friend there to meet me," Elizabeth recalled.

Father and daughter went on to Portland, where he bought the fruit trees. On the way back they stopped at Mr. Dodd's. "Mr. Holtgrieve was there and he and Father talked the matter over and said he would be up the next week to our place to marry me."

In fact they were married, the groom twenty-eight and the bride fourteen. Elizabeth never said what she thought of "Mr. Holtgrieve," but they had eight children and stayed married until he died.[2]

For other couples, the courtship was more prolonged and more fun. "In July, 1853, some young men from Yreka brought saddle horses and invited us girls to take a trip to Yreka, where they were going to have a big dance," said Mary Dunn, who came to the Willamette Valley when she was sixteen. "We started at nine in the morning, rode over the Siskiyous over the trail, and reached Yreka at sunset. The streets were lined with miners who had heard we were coming and wanted to see us. We stayed at my Aunt Louise

A typical dance hall in the 1870s

Kelly's for several days and it was a continuous reception all the time we were there."

Mary left with a lifetime memento of the dance. "A young jeweler gave me a pair of ear-rings he made from Yreka gold dust. He pierced my ears and put the ear-rings in. That was 75 years ago, and I have never had them out of my ears since," she told a newspaper columnist in 1927.[3]

Because there were so many eligible men, young women could be choosy. "You stated that Edward C was a coming out here in the spring & that he intends to have one of Fathers girls," Rachel Malick wrote home to her sister in Illinois. "As for that I don't know but as for my self he shal not get [me] because I wont have him, nor mr. Phiester wont get me [either]. Although as far as I know they both are very respectable young men but they dont suit my taste."[4] Instead Rachel had her pick of young soldiers who were stationed just a mile from her home, at Fort Vancouver.

The husband Rachel chose, John Biles, made a positive impression on her mother. "He is Avery good work Man. . . . His traid is A wagon And Coach-maker. And he can make all kind of furneture. And he is Avery in dustru[ous] young Man and is well be loved by All hoo knos him."

Besides these admirable virtues, Mrs. Malick noticed that he was also "very handsom. He has blue eyes And light hair And is very pretty spoken. He dose not Sware nore Spake eney bad wordes And is A butiful form. Nore he does not drink nor play cards nor is not guiltey of eney bad habits what ever And is very saving. I think that he will Make Avery good husband for hooever gets him."[5]

Men, too, were looking for wives who were more than pretty. R. R. Rees wrote to Augusta Ward in Portland in 1863 pleading his case for marriage. He did not want a woman who would be "the beauty of the ballroom," he wrote, but "'the darling of my own home, the tidiest of them all,' a woman competent to superintend such a place, and one who would study her husband's best interest in superintending it." He added that "I have a fondness for good dinners, and could love the individual equally well who cooked them."[6]

Even with choices, however, some young women married for desperate reasons. Matilda Jane Sager had lived most of her early life in terror. She was five when her family traveled to Oregon in 1844, but both parents died of mountain fever on the way. Matilda and her six siblings were left at the Whitman Mission in Waiilatpu. When the Whitmans and two of the Sager brothers were killed in a massacre, Matilda was ransomed from the Indians and placed with various families. Most did not treat her well.

"From the time I was eight until I was 15 I was whipped so much that I got to feeling about it as one does the winter rain—that it was inevitable and was to be borne without complaint. . . .

"I was whipped so much that the neighbors finally complained and they had me summoned to give evidence before the judge. The man I lived with said the neighbors should mind their own business and, that he could discipline me more effectively if the judge would bind me out to him till I was sixteen." The judge was willing, but there was a dispute about Matilda's age, and she didn't wait to hear the outcome.

"While they were settling that I married a miner from Shasta County, California, and went to the gold mines with him."[7]

Rachel Malick's marriage began on a better note. The pattern for her wedding dress came from England by steamer to San Francisco and then up to Vancouver. "In this letter I will enclose some of My white Matrimonial Robe but I haint Maryed yet," she wrote to her sister in 1852. "I can't send you any of the flowerd part in the same letter but the flowerd part is around the botom of my dress. All Flowerd in white up as high as the waist Almost."[8]

There were forty guests at their wedding, and Rachel sent a small piece of the wedding cake back to Illinois. "I am Maryed to Mr. John D. Biles," and "everybody says we were the Pretyest Couple They ever saw. . . ." John built a house, they made a garden, and moved into the house in October. "We have everything fixed very nice. . . .

This wedding dress was worn by a well-to-do bride in 1850.

My husband . . . is very kind to me in every respect. . . . We have plenty to eat, drink and wear and every thing in pleanty. . . ."[9]

Not all new brides were so nicely settled. Women who came with their husbands in the army found living conditions rough. Frances Grummond described the first breakfast she cooked while camping in tents at Fort Phil Kearney in Wyoming after a snowfall during the night. The bacon and coffee turned out all right, but her biscuits were made from flour, salt, and water and were as hard as stones.

"No hatchet chanced to be conveniently near to aid in separating them in halves . . . ," she wrote. "Impulsively I seized the butcher knife, but in the endeavor to do hatchet-work with it, the blade slipped and almost severed my thumb, mingling both blood and tears."[10]

Young women like Frances did not remain "brides" very long. Her husband was killed in a clash with Indians shortly after they were married. Rachel Malick Biles died at nineteen, attempting to give birth to twins.

The term *bride* hardly fit an environment where both adults worked constantly merely to survive. "My mother bore 12 children, worked hard all her life, and died a comparatively young woman," Marianne Hunsaker Edwards D'Arcy recalled. "It usually was the second or third wife that enjoyed the improved farm and the comforts that the first and second wives had worked so hard to help earn."[11]

5

MIDWIVES

Many new brides found that pregnancy and childbirth were not nearly as much fun as the courtship had been. "I do think a pregnant woman has a hard time of it," remarked Susan Magoffin in Santa Fe. "Some sickness all the time, heart-burn, headache, cramp, etc., after all this thing of marrying is not what it is cracked up to be."[1]

Yet pregnancy and childbirth were considered routine; no reason to slow down a wagon train or call in a doctor, even if there was one. One day was long enough to stop. Then mother and baby bumped along with the rest of the train as it moved over rough land.

Lydia Waters remembered the birth of a child on a journey to California in 1855. The wagon train halted in the afternoon for the birth, but Indians had been threatening the train in the morning. When several warriors rode in close to the stopped wagons, someone made the sign for smallpox, and they withdrew.

Meanwhile, "the mother of the woman who was confined cried and cried, fearing her daughter would die. Then the others followed suit, and so, as usual when there was trouble, I had to boss the job," Waters related. Her "bossing" must have helped. "We laid over one day, and then moved on. The mother and child did well, could not have done better anywhere else."[2]

Once settled in the West, women could at least stay in

A wagon train usually halted only briefly when a baby was born.

one place when a baby was born. On frontier farms, however, help in childbirth—someone to boss the job—might be miles away. Medical care was simply the nearest female neighbor, if she got there in time.

"On New Year's morning, 1842, my father got up at about daybreak and built the fire," recalled Marianne Hunsaker. "My parents were living in a log cabin that had not yet been chinked. Father said some of the logs were crooked, which resulted in making chinks large enough to throw a cat through, providing the cat was not too large. The snow had sifted in upon the floor. As he turned to get the broom to sweep out the freshly fallen snow from the floor he saw that Mother was awake, so he said, 'New Year's gift, Emily.'

"She said, 'You had better hurry over to our neighbor's and bring her back with you or I will have a New Year's gift for you while you are gone.' He hurried into coat and cap and went for the neighbor. Shortly after her arrival I also arrived, so Mother made good on her promise of presenting Father with a New Year's gift."[3]

Gradually, in isolated communities, one woman became known as a "midwife." Through necessity and experience, she learned how to make herbal remedies, set bones, and deliver babies. Sometimes the only medical "training" she had was what she read from a book.

"The health of a people in a new country is usually good, but we would sometimes get sick," recounted an early pioneer. "Would hardly dare think of sending for a doctor. There was no money to pay one and there could hardly be one found. But there was a woman who lived in our neighborhood that had a good doctor book. It was Doctor Gunn's work. She went by it in her own family, and the neighbors sent for her. She would take her doctor book under her arm and go to visit the sick. Then they would read and study together and use the simple remedies prescribed in that book and get along pretty well. In that way she got into quite a large practice."

Besides nursing the sick, the woman who read Doctor Gunn's book assisted at more than a hundred births. "She was very successful, never lost a mother or child while she was taking care of them. She most always went back every day for a week to see the patient and wash and dress the baby."[4]

In Colorado in the 1870s, Attie Long Thompson remembered a midwife named Nancy Ann Roberts. "She was a big fat woman who smoked a corn-cob pipe, and could swear like a man. Her face was always sunburned because she never wore anything on her head. She combed her hair, what little she had, straight back and twisted it on top of her head into a knot about as large as a good sized button. Her neck was always dirty, as well as her dress and apron, and her ranch was called 'The Dirty Woman's Ranch.'"

Despite the dirt, "Ma sent for Nancy Ann when she knew her time had come. She came striding into the room and taking her pipe out of her mouth said, 'Damn it, Mrs. Long, when are you going to stop havin young'ens?'"

The children were sent outdoors to play, sliding down the haystack, until "Pa called us in and we were shown the new baby. . . . Nancy Ann left a generous supply of catnip tea, in case the baby had the colic and also left some saffron tea to give it to whiten its skin."[5] (Perhaps the baby had jaundice, a common ailment just after birth in which the skin turns slightly yellow.)

In the Arizona mining town of Mascot, Dolores Lopez Montoya ran a boardinghouse and also served as a midwife, or *partera*. "Whatever babies were born in Mascot, she delivered them," her daughter Esperanza recounted. "Anyone that needed help would come to her. If they were sick, or if their babies were sick, they came to her for advice. She gave them medicines and comforted them."[6] Montoya also gave the babies tea when they had indigestion and colic.

If no women were available, husbands were called on to help. A Japanese immigrant, Gin Okazaki, recalled that "in every family the husband played the role of midwife. My husband had had no experience as a midwife, but he had a friend who had once helped in an emergency and had safely delivered the baby, so my husband went to him to ask how he did it.

"'The important thing is how to cut the umbilical cord. First you tie it tightly with string in two places. Then cut it between the tied places with a pair of scissors.'

"When the time came, my husband and I, one way or another, cut the cord and delivered a beautiful baby."[7]

Without trained medical care, women and babies sometimes died during childbirth, events that saddened but did not slow down the westward movement. On the desert trail to California in the gold rush of 1849, Catherine Hunn wrote about a woman named Mrs. Lamore who had died in childbirth, leaving a husband and two small daughters. "We halted a day to bury her and the infant that had lived but an hour in this weird, lonely spot of God's footstool away apparently from everywhere and everybody. . . .

"There was no tombstone—why should there be—the poor husband and orphans could never hope to revisit the grave and to the world it was just one of the many hundreds that marked the trail. . . ."[8]

If the mother died in childbirth or had no breast milk, the baby was immediately in danger. On the coast, clam juice was used as a substitute. Elsewhere, a nursing mother had to be found. Henrietta Sager was only five months old when her mother died on the Oregon Trail, so "Henrietta was passed from one mother to another, wherever there was a mother who had a baby about her age."[9] When missionary Mary Richardson Walker had a very painful time nursing, an Indian woman was found who would nurse the baby.

Despite the hardships and also because of them, children on the frontier were a blessing. The birth of a child was a significant event, and, like the wedding cake, mementos were sent back east. Her son, Charles, was one of the "prettiest boys in existence," Rachel Biles wrote to her sister. "He has blue eyes and light hair. . . . I will put a little of it in this letter so you and the children can see it."[10]

"If I were near you I could tell you so many of her little winning ways, and how very pretty and cunning she was," wrote Susanna Townsend after the birth of her daughter. "You ought to have seen Emory delight when he saw her first intelligent smile bestowed upon him. . . . Bless her little heart he exclaimed she is smiling at me. . . ."

The Townsends' daughter lived only four months, but she provided companionship to parents who seldom saw anyone else: "Of course being only four months when she died her faculties were not greatly developed, but I talked to her so much she came already to understand a good deal, and she talked to me with her countenance."[11]

As if to compensate for frequent deaths among children, couples had large families. Mrs. George Applin recalled, "When I was young we took what the good God sent, without complaint."[12] She had thirteen children.

"Father and Mother had twelve children," recounted Laura Million Howard. "Six of us were born before they came across the plains, and the other six were born here in Oregon. There were seven girls and five boys in our family. They always used to say that Father was pretty well fixed, with seven Million girls and five Million boys."[13]

If they survived infancy, children still faced dangers from wagon wheels, boiling pots, gun accidents, and wild animals. Even cattle could be dangerous. "In those days [1848] the entire country was unfenced," remembered Laura Caldwell in Oregon. "Tom Owens had some wild cattle that roamed all over the country. These Spanish cattle were as fleet and as wild as a deer. It was dangerous to be caught out on foot when a band of these cattle were around.

"The schoolhouse was two miles from our house. My sister, Angelica, was about three and a half years old and I was seven years old. Mother had made Angelica a new dress out of bright red cloth. When we were about a mile from home and the same distance from the schoolhouse, I saw the cattle beginning to gather toward us. Father had told me that in case of danger always stand my ground and never to run. Taking Angelica by the hand I told her to stand perfectly still. From all directions the cattle began running up until they had formed a circle around us. They put their heads down close to the ground and bawled and pawed the ground. They pressed closer and closer until I could almost touch their horns by putting my hands out. They sniffed and smelled at us and snorted, but we stood as still as two little mice, and finally the cattle went away. I am sure that if we had started to run we would have been pawed to death and trampled into the earth."[14]

Guns were always around, for both hunting and protection. "When my brother George was eight years old he got hold of Cousin Israel's gun and said he would show my sister and myself how to shoot it," Laura also recalled. "He didn't know it was loaded, but it was, so he pulled the trigger and it went off with a terrific roar. I screamed. The squaws ran to where we were and Mother rushed out and said, 'Are you hurt?'

"I said, 'I am shot.'

"She said, 'Where are you shot?'

"I said, 'I am shot through the head. The gun nearly killed my ears.'"[15]

Diseases also spread among the communities. "When I was a girl we knew but little about the danger of contagious diseases," said Marianne Hunsaker Edwards D'Arcy. "When a child had what they called putrid sore throat the neighbors all came with their children to visit, and when the child died, as it frequently did, the neighbors for miles around came to the funeral and took the germs of diphtheria home to their children, and the minister was kept busy preaching funeral sermons for the children of the neighborhood.[16]

Gradually, the standards of health care improved and children lived longer. A Mormon midwife, Patty Sessions, had accompanied Brigham Young's wagon train from Nauvoo to Salt Lake City, and she continually urged other women to go to medical school. One who did was Ellis Reynolds Shipp.

At the age of twenty-eight, already the mother of five

children, she went to the Women's Medical College of Pennsylvania and returned to a practice with "special attention given to obstetrics, diseases of women, and minor surgery." Ellis Shipp's care of a new mother went well beyond just delivering the baby. It included "ten visits after the birth when she would bathe mother and infant, make the bed, and sometimes cook a bowl of gruel if the mother's appetite failed; in fact, she did anything she could do for the comfort and well-being of her patient"—all for $25—"when it was convenient."[17]

In a difficult childbirth, a doctor could be a lifesaver. Susanna Townsend's first child had been stillborn, but she benefited from the presence of a doctor for the second. "I had no idea from my former experience that a Dr. could render so much assistance to a woman in that fearful hour. I believe that with no better aid than I had before my little one would have shared the fate of her brother. As it was her life was doubtful for a few minutes." The child had no pulse, but the doctor left the umbilical cord attached, and circulation was restored "after a few very anxious minutes."[18]

Still, having a doctor at a birth was a real luxury. "My last baby was a little 13-pound boy," recounted Helen Olson Halvorsen, who had served as a midwife herself. "I seemed so free from worry! I had a doctor for the first time. Dad was about half provoked when I sent for the doctor, though. Well, I suppose it did seem like a waste of money when I had seven without a doctor, and without putting anybody to much extra trouble or expense."[19]

6

NEIGHBORS

If men missed the company of women on the frontier, so did women miss the company of other women. Emigrants leaving for the West knew they might never see relatives and friends again. Narcissa Whitman cut off a lock of her hair to leave with a female friend. It was two years and five months before the first letter from "home" reached her in the Oregon Territory.

"Every good woman needs a companion of her own sex, no matter how numerous or valuable her male acquaintants, no matter how close the union between herself and husband," wrote Georgiana Bruce Kirby when she had a falling out with a friend in Santa Cruz.[1]

When the McDaniel family arrived in Grass Valley, California, a woman named Mrs. Shelton rushed out from her boardinghouse to greet them. "She helped mother out of the wagon and as mother got down from her high seat, she was embraced affectionately as though she had been a long lost sister," wrote young Kate McDaniel. "This poor, pioneer woman was overjoyed to see another woman come into the camp and she said, 'Oh, my dear, you seem just like an angel come to me in my loneliness.'"[2]

The first neighbors of the early settlers were Hudson's Bay Company men and the Native Americans. To plant their first wheat, recounted Sara McAllister Hartman, "father secured a half bushel through the kindness of an old English gentleman." The gentleman was probably John McLoughlin, the chief factor at Fort Vancouver, who was well known for his generosity to early settlers. "The other families procured the same quantity and were obliged to plant and re-plant for three years before they dared to use any, and during those three years the five families never saw bread, let alone tasting it."

A trading post carried supplies needed by the early settlers, such as tools, traps, seed, and weapons.

With the help of the Native Americans, however, they always had plenty to eat, "all kinds of game, which was more plentiful than tame stock now, fish and clams, dried and fresh, the Indians showing us how to prepare them. . . .

"To our elders it must have been quite a hardship, but the children did not know the want of it [wheat bread] and was happy and healthy without it. We had fern-root bread, which amply filled its place. . . . Our squaw nurse trained us to eat Indian food, strictly following the Indians course and preparations of food, and a more hearty, healthful, happy lot of children would be hard to find in any land."[3]

In Oregon, too, Rhoda Quick Johnson's family received help. "The Indians were mighty good to the whites when we came here. They used to bring us clams, salmon, game, and big bladders of whale oil for our lamps. The whales would strand on the shore and the Indians would try out their blubber. The men folks would give the Indians a chisel or an ax head as a present, in exchange for the things they brought us."[4]

As the Indian women shared their knowledge of edible plants, they were also curious about the emigrant women. The feeling of being constantly watched could be uncomfortable. "I scarcely do anything from morning till night without being seen by some of them," wrote missionary Mary Walker in her diary. "Sometimes I feel . . . I cannot endure it any longer. . . ."[5]

Indian men, especially, came into cabins unasked and expected to share the food, as was their custom. "One day as mother was cooking hoecakes by the fire, one old fellow squatted down as close to her Dutch oven as [he] could get," wrote Sara McAllister. "Mother stepped out for a moment, and when she returned she missed her cakes. She noticed the old fellow holding his arms out in a suspicious manner. Suspecting the trouble, she stepped up to him, took hold of his arms and pressed them to his sides, holding them like a vise, burning his arms to a blister. The old rascal had stolen mother's cake and hidden it under his blanket. He was known afterwards as Old Hoecake."[6]

Despite times when neighbors were too friendly, neighborliness was a survival habit. The common enemy was starvation. "This country was covered with bunchgrass, flowers, Indians, coyotes, and grasshoppers," said Mrs. Brewster Ferrel of the Walla Walla Valley in Washington Territory in the 1860s. "A few white people were living along the creeks in little huts. Some were growing a little wheat and others small grain and gardens. Everything was very high priced. . . ." One neighbor was living on boiled wheat.

Mrs. Ferrel saw a positive side to the hardship: "Those hard times seemed to bind neighbors close together. Three or four of us would get together and go two or three miles to get some wild gooseberries and elderberries and red haws and fix them up for fruit. They were pretty good when there was nothing better."[7]

It was not only food that was shared but some of the smaller comforts. Bethenia Owens-Adair, the first woman doctor in the West, remembered when her mother was grateful for a gift of rags. "I think the most unhappy period of my life was the first year spent on Clatsop, simply for the want of something to do," her mother had written. "I had no yarn to knit, nothing to sew, not even rags to make patches. We had very little to cook. Salmon and potatoes were our principal diet. One of my greatest needs was a

Dr. Bethenia Owens-Adair was the first woman doctor in Oregon.

cloth for a dish rag. One day Mrs. Parrish [a neighbor] gave me a sack full of rags and I never received a present before nor since that I so highly appreciated as I did those rags."[8]

For a young bride, advice was what was needed. Socorro Félix Delgado's grandmother was a bride of sixteen or seventeen, on the King's Ranch in Arizona in the late 1880s. "She had been the smallest in the family . . . and she didn't know how to cook or wash or do anything," so she would go and talk to wives of other *vaqueros*, or cowboys, "but she was also very proud and independent and didn't like to admit that she didn't know how to cook.

"She would say, 'And how do you make *albondigas* [meatball soup]? How do you make this? How do you make that?'

"'Well, there's nothing to it,' they would tell her. 'Everybody does it the same way.'

"'Yes, but how do you make them?' she would ask, and then she would run to her house and write it down before she forgot it."[9]

Sharing food, rags, and advice, neighbors were also a great comfort in sickness, and sometimes the difference between life and death. "When there was any sickness in the country," wrote Attie Thompson of her mother, "she was usually sent for and it did not matter how far she had to go, whether it was day or night, the weather warm or cold, she would always go and stay until the person was well. . . . Sometimes she would receive five dollars for her trouble, but, if the patient happened to be a neighbor, she would receive nothing, because they would expect to return the kindness someday."[10]

Midwives were called on to set bones, treat burns, and provide simple herbal remedies. They used cobwebs to stop bleeding, wet dirt or vegetable parings to soothe bites and stings, and various poultices made of wheat flour and salt or bread and milk to treat almost anything. For tonsillitis, salt pork was chopped up with onions; for a cold, an onion syrup was made or a cough syrup of egg whites thickened in vinegar.

Esperanza Montoya Padilla remembers that her grandmother "had all kinds of little jars with herbs. . . . She also gave massages to everyone who was sick. She made this stuff that was so stinky from turpentine and I don't know what in the world! It smelled worse than Ben Gay."[11]

When neighbors did not look out for each other, tragedy could result. Luzena Wilson was living in Sacramento in tents during the mining rush, working hard and hurrying all day, tired out. She grew hard-hearted, "but I might have stopped sometimes for a minute to heed the moans which caught my ears from the canvas house next to me." She knew a young man lived there, for he had often stopped to say good morning, but she thought he had other friends in the town. She heard his weak calls for water and assumed someone else gave it to him. "One day the moans ceased, and, on looking in, I found him lying dead with not even a friendly hand to close his eyes." She sorely regretted her neglect.[12]

Even when it was needed, help was sometimes hard to ask for—pioneers were used to being self-sufficient. Mary Jane Cooness Washington was the wife of a black man named George Washington, who founded the town of Centralia, Washington. She had learned from a man that his family, including four or five children, had gone without food for more than a day.

"Then my mother got really angry, angrier than I'd ever known her to be, and the only time I've ever seen her so since she professed Christianity," recounted her son, Stacey. "She always baked a pan of biscuits two feet square every morning and it lasted the three of us for two meals. She had breakfast already cooked—biscuits, eggs, bacon, and mashed potatoes. She put the pan of biscuits in a clean pillowslip, put the mashed potatoes in a bowl and the eggs on top of it. Then as she gave him these things and sugar and coffee and a jar of milk, she said, 'Why did you let things go so long when you knew you could always come to us? You take this to Mary and the children and then come back and I'll have breakfast ready for you by the time you get here.'"[13]

With kindly neighbors, hardship could be endured. Without them, loneliness prevailed. "My grandmother told me that the Baboquivari [where she lived] was a very lonely place," recounted Socorro Delgado. "She was so young and she was afraid. My grandfather would leave early in the morning and come back late at night while they were herding cattle."[14]

In the Yakima Valley of Washington, Teiko Matsui Tomita expressed her loneliness in tanka:

> Neighbors are five miles far away
> Many days without seeing anyone
> Today, too, without seeing anyone
> The sun sets.[15]

WOMEN ON THEIR OWN

Death at a young age was common in the West, a part of daily life. Babies and children died from disease and accidents; men and women died from disease, childbearing, accidents, and conflicts. Many women became widows before they ever reached the West.

Cholera, an illness that causes severe diarrhea and cramps, first struck the pioneers on the wagon trains in a serious epidemic in 1849. Five thousand died that year as the illness spread through contaminated water. Smallpox, malaria, and ailments the pioneers called "ague," "mountain fever," and "bilious fever" could also be fatal.

"Two days before we came to Chimney Rock the cholera struck us," remembered Marilla R. Washburn Bailey. "Seven died in our train that night and four the next day. A young man in our wagon train named Hyde went out as a guard for the stock that night. When he left, after supper, he seemed perfectly well. When the guard was changed at midnight Mr. Wood brought his body back to the train. He had been taken with severe cramps and died within two hours."

Marilla herself was lucky. "My brother and I both took the cholera. Mother gave us all the hot whiskey she could pour down us and put flannel cloths soaked in whiskey, as hot as we could bear them, on our stomachs. This cured us."[1]

When a husband died, his widow had little time to grieve. She had to make quick decisions about how she would take care of her family. A "desolate looking group," a woman and her five children, were found by the trail on the way to the California goldfields in 1852.

Graves along the Oregon Trail

"An open, bleak prairie, the cold wind howling over-head, bearing with it the mournful tones of that deserted woman; a new made grave, a woman and three children sitting near by; a girl of fourteen summers walking round and round in a circle, wringing her hands and calling upon her dead parent; a boy of twelve sitting upon the wagon tongue, sobbing aloud; a strange man placing a rude head-board at the head of the grave; the oxen feeding nearby. . . .

"We stopped to look upon the scene and asked the woman if we could be of any service," wrote a traveler who passed by them soon after the death of the father.

"'I need nothing,' she replied, 'but advice—whether I shall pursue my journey or go back to my old home in Illinois.'"[2]

Many widows chose to go on, particularly if they were part of a wagon train. When Elvina Apperson Fellows's father died crossing the plains, her mother prepared to proceed. "We had two wagons, so Mother had the men take the wagon bed of one of them to make a coffin. She abandoned the running gear, ox yokes, and some of our outfit, and we finished the trip with one wagon."[3]

Although they had set off for the West with high hopes, when families were diminished by death, daily life became a mere struggle to survive. Only fierce determination or the help of neighbors would stave off starvation. Louise Clappe described the look on the face of one woman whose husband had died of cholera, leaving her with eight sons and one daughter.

"She had come on; for what else could she do. . . . She was immensely tall, and had a hard, weather-beaten face, surmounted by a dreadful horn comb and a heavy twist of haycolored hair, which, before it was cut, and its gloss all destroyed by the alkali, must, from its luxuriance, have been very handsome. But what really interested me so much in her was the dogged and determined way in which she had set that stern, wrinkled face of hers against poverty. She owned nothing in the world but her team, and yet she planned all sorts of successful ways to get food for her small, or rather large, family."

The woman with the stern face washed shirts and ironed them on a chair in the open air, and the men in the mining camps paid her three or four times as much as she asked. "She accumulated quite a handsome sum in a few days. She made me think of a long-legged very thin hen scratching for dear life to feed her never-to-be-satisfied brood."[4]

Physical strength, good health, and a certain "nimbleness" also worked in a woman's favor, as described by Elizabeth Geer, mother of seven. "I will not attempt to describe my troubles since I saw you," she wrote to a friend back East. "Suffice it to say, I was left a widow in a foreign land without one solitary friend. . . . I became as poor as a snake, yet I was in good health, and never so nimble since I was a child."[5]

Staying on the land was one choice for a widow. If she and her husband had already staked a claim, under the Donation Land Claim Act, she had to stay on the land to keep it. Charles Clark's father had been greatly impressed with a piece of land in Washington Territory near the Walla Walla Valley in 1859. After making his claim, he sowed oats and planted fruit trees. When he journeyed to Portland, however, to bring his wife and two-year-old son to the claim, he became ill suddenly and died.

Charles's mother continued on by steamer and army

ambulance. "As you can imagine it was a sad, hard journey for a woman who had just been made a widow and who was soon to be again a mother," he recalled. She was strongly advised to give up the claim, and a man offered her $300 for it, but she was determined to hold on.

After a two-week stay, she returned to Portland, but twelve-year-old Charles stayed on to work the claim. "I spent that summer, sometimes a very lonesome one, in the tent, or hoeing the garden which he had put out." In September, with help from two adult male friends, a log cabin was built. His mother came back to Walla Walla in October with a six-week-old baby and lived the rest of her life there.

"During those early years the valley seemed to be filled with Indians, but they were very kindly and well disposed, and we had no trouble with them, even though a good part of the time we were alone, mother and the baby and the little boy and myself as the nearest a man about the place. We had plenty of horses and cattle and chickens and garden and had an abundance of necessities, though no elegancies.

"During the long, cold nights of winter in 1860–61 we lived alone in our cabin. Mother and I would grind our flour in the big coffee-mill. One regular job we had, and often we were up till midnight working at it, and that was to make sacks for the flour-mill. . . ."[6]

Farming, making flour sacks, taking in laundry, opening a boardinghouse—these were the kinds of work women and their children could find. After reaching Portland with one wagon, Elvina Fellows continued the family's story. "Mother had no money and had nine hungry mouths to fill in addition to her own, so she would go to the ships that came and get washing to do. She soon had all the washing she could handle, and so we got along. Then she started a boarding house."[7]

Women often had plenty of practice being self-sufficient. In 1848, many men were lured from their farms

A widow might earn a living by doing laundry for others.

to the gold rush in California, hoping to become rich quickly and return home. Sara McAllister's father left the farm and small shingle mill he had been running, using the resources of the forest. "While he was absent," she recounted, "someone sent an order for shingles; mother would not lose the order, so she hired a crew and filled the demand, making about five hundred dollars."[8]

On farms and ranches, a woman might continue to live on the land. In the towns and cities, domestic service was a possibility. There was no shame attached to a poor woman earning an honest living as a housemaid, cook, nursemaid, or nurse, recalled Theresa Dixon Flowers. Her mother, also named Theresa, had been brought as a young girl to Astoria, Oregon, with a white family from Georgia. She had trained as a nurse, but when she married she ran an oyster house with her husband instead. When the local railroad collapsed and that business failed, she returned to nursing.

"My father had an accident and she had to go to work. She had had nurses training in Vancouver, so she did nursing and then she did midwifery. . . . She worked for many years. I know times when she wouldn't get home to stay for a year. She'd go from one case to another."[9]

Widows could often remarry, but some were not so eager to give up the single life. Pauline Lyon Williamson came out to Oakland, California, from Plainfield, New Jersey, with her small son in 1855. She planned to live with her aunt and uncle while working in a hospital training program, but she discovered they had already planned a marriage for her. After foiling their plan, "I told him [her aunt's friend] I did not care to marry, but he assured me I would marry out here, [since] every one that came to make

Theresa Townes was born in 1858 in Georgia. She came to Astoria by boat and later married Roscoe Dixon.

a living ended by marrying. . . . He kept it up so much that I finally told [him] I did not see why people worried so much about my getting married. I came to earn a living and not to hunt a husband, and I intended to remain single."[10]

On the other hand, supporting self and children could be a lonely life. "Mother got tired of trying to meet life alone, so she married an old man who lived at Oregon City," Elvina Fellows continued her mother's story. Long before she remarried, however, Elvina's mother had been in desperate straits. "In 1851 Mother was pretty hard run to earn enough money for us to live on, so when a man named Julius Thomas, a cook in a restaurant, offered to marry me, Mother thought I had better take him, so I did. He was 44 and I was 14."

What did the young bride think of this? She compared it to slavery. "Back in 1851 . . . we had slavery of Negroes in the South, and we had slavery of wives all over the United States, and saloons wherever there were enough people to make running one pay. What could a girl of 14 do to protect herself from a man of 44, particularly if he drank most of the time, as my husband did?. . . When he was drunk he often wanted to kill me, and he used to beat me until I thought I couldn't stand it."

Fortunately, Elvina herself became a widow. "One time he came to my mother's house, where I had taken refuge. I locked the door. He tried to climb in at the window, but I held it down. This enraged him so, he took out his pistol and shot at me. The bullet passed just above my head. The glass fell on me and scared me so I dropped to the floor." When her husband saw her lying on the floor, he thought he had killed her and so he killed himself, "and I was a widow."[11]

Such brutal experiences molded tough, independent women. Women who faced new challenges constantly, who could not avoid hard work and loneliness, felt no obligation to defer to men. Among the band of missionaries who came west in the 1830s, some men objected to women praying aloud in public. Narcissa Whitman had no patience with such an attitude.

Her own attitude was more like that of Dr. Bethenia Owens-Adair, who "thought she could do anything a boy could, and was just as good and maybe a little better."[12]

Even Ellis Reynolds Shipp, whose religion told her to accept other wives in a polygamous marriage, had the self-confidence and gumption to become the second female doctor in Utah. Indeed her fellow wives took care of her children when she went to Philadelphia for training at the first Women's Medical College in the United States.

The resourcefulness and independence required of women on the frontier led them to demand rights their eastern sisters more slowly acquired. The newness and less-established nature of the West seemed to allow more freedom. When the activist Susan B. Anthony came west on a national speaking tour in 1871, women flocked to hear her. Seven years later the Oregon legislature gave married women the right to own, sell, or will property and to keep their own wages.

As they wrote constitutions, western territories and states were the first to give women the right to vote: Wyoming, 1859; Utah, 1870 (abolished by Congress in 1887 but reenacted in 1896); Washington, 1883 (voided in 1887, passed again in 1910); Colorado, 1893; Idaho, 1896; Oregon, 1912.

Nevertheless, the pioneer life took a heavy toll. Narcissa Whitman was very unhappy, and Mary Richardson Walker eventually lost her mind. In her old age she sat for hours on a wooden horse, rocking and reliving the journey west.

"I am 87 years old," said Marilla Bailey in 1926. "I was married at 15, and was not only a good cook and housekeeper, but I knew how to take care of babies, from having cared for my brothers and sisters. I had ten babies of my own and never had help. I could paddle my canoe on the river or handle the oars in a rowboat as well as an Indian.

Susan B. Anthony was active in the woman suffrage movement from about 1850. This photo was taken in her later years.

When my husband was away I could rustle the meat on which we lived, for I could handle a revolver or rifle as well as most men.

"During the early days I lived in tents, in log pens, and in log cabins. The modern mother would think twice before she let her 15-year-old daughter move out on a tract of timber, miles away from any other settler, where she would have to kill the game for meat, cook over a fireplace, take care of the children, make soap and make clothes for the children.

"Sometimes I wonder if the girl of today is as self-reliant, self-sacrificing and as useful as girls were when I was a girl. . . .They have liberty that in our day was undreamed of. . . ."[13]

She may wonder. Yet the spirit of these pioneer women—the hopeful bride on her way to "heaven," the neighbor who expected to "return the kindness," the widow who set her face against poverty, and the girl who thought "she could do anything a boy could"—surely flourishes today in the descendants of these remarkable western pioneers.

SOURCE NOTES

INTRODUCTION

1. Dee Brown, *Gentle Tamers: Women in the Old Wild West* (Lincoln: University of Nebraska Press, 1968), 16.

2. Nancy Wilson Ross, *Westward the Women* (New York: Knopf, 1944), 110.

3. JoAnn Levy, *They Saw the Elephant: Women in the California Gold Rush* (Hamden, Conn.: Archon Books, 1990), 178.

4. Brown, *Gentle Tamers*, 220.

5. Caroline Leighton, *Life at Puget Sound* (Fairfield, Wash.: Ye Galleon Press, 1979), 221.

6. Brown, *Gentle Tamers*, 16.

7. Leighton, *Life at Puget Sound*, 103.

8. Ross, *Westward the Women*, 111.

9. Levy, *They Saw the Elephant*, 175.

10. Ibid., 116.

11. Lillian Schlissel, Byrd Gibbens, and Elizabeth Hampsten, *Far from Home: Families of the Westward Journey* (New York: Shocken, 1989), 16.

1. THE FIRST WOMEN

1. This excerpt is reprinted with permission of the publisher from *Strangers in Blood: Fur Trade Company Families in Indian Country* by Jennifer Brown (Vancouver: University of British Columbia Press), 1980. All rights reserved by the Publisher.

2. Ross, *Westward the Women*, 15.

3. Brown, *Gentle Tamers*, 212–213.

4. Cathy Luchetti and Carol Olwell, *Women of the West* (Berkeley: Antelope Island Press, 1982), 104–105.

5. Archie Binns, *Peter Skene Ogden: Fur Trader* (Portland, Ore.: Binford and Mort, 1967), 98.

6. Brown, *Gentle Tamers*, 212.

7. Binns, *Peter Skene Ogden*, 57.

8. Alberta Brooks Fogdall, *Royal Family of the Columbia: Dr. John McLoughlin and His Family* (Fairfield, Wash.: Ye Galleon Press, 1978), 123.

9. Leighton, *Life at Puget Sound*, 76.

10. Brown, *Strangers in Blood*.

11. Ibid.

12. *Tsagigla'lal: She Who Watches*, Washington Women, A Centennial Celebration, vol. 1, June 1992. Compiled and written by Jennifer James Wilson and Brenda Owings-Klimek (Olympia, Wash.: Office of Superintendent of Public Instruction, 1989), 9.

2. THE INVISIBLE WOMEN

1. Ross, *Westward the Women*, 122–129.

2. Levy, *They Saw the Elephant*, 150.

3. Doreen Rappaport, ed., *American Women: Their Lives in Their Words* (New York: HarperCollins, 1992), 140.

4. Kazuo Ito, *Issei: A History of Japanese Immigrants in North America* (Seattle: Executive Committee for Publication of Issei, 1976), 771.

5. Ibid., 765.

6. Ross, *Westward the Women*, 129–130.

3. MARRIAGES OF CONVENIENCE

1. Ross, *Westward the Women*, 24.

2. Ibid., 57.

3. Clifford Merrill Drury, *Elkanah and Mary Walker: Pioneers Among the Spokanes* (Caldwell, Idaho: Caxton Printers, 1940), 68–69.

4. Ross, *Westward the Women*, 137.

5. Fred Lockley, *Conversations with Pioneer Women*. Compiled and edited by Michael Helm. (Eugene, Ore.: Rainy Day Press, 1981), 250.

6. Brown, *Gentle Tamers*, 227.

7. Levy, *They Saw the Elephant*, 173.

8. Brown, *Gentle Tamers*, 229.

9. *Tsagigla'lal*, 85.

10. Atlanta Georgia Long Thompson, *Daughter of a Pioneer: A True Story of Life in Early Colorado* (Portland, Ore. Binford and Mort, 1982), 73.

11. *Tsagigla'lal*, 79.

12. Roger Conant, *Mercer's Belles* (Seattle: University of Washington Press, 1960), 10.

13. *Tsagigla'lal*, 76–77.

14. Ann S. Conner Hartsuck Papers, University of Washington Libraries.

15. Conant, *Mercer's Belles*, 129.

16. Ibid., 136.

17. Ibid., 131.

18. Ibid., 145.

19. Ron Strickland, *River Pigs and Cayuses* (San Francisco: Lexikos, 1984), 21.

20. Ito, *Issei,* 192.

21. Ibid., 249.

22. Ibid., 247–248.

23. *Tsagigla'lal,* 96.

4. LOVE AND MARRIAGE

1. Lockley, *Conversations with Pioneer Women,* 251.

2. Ibid., 160.

3. Ibid., 74.

4. Schlissel et al., *Far from Home,* 16.

5. Ibid., 20.

6. Robert Allen Bennett, *We'll All Go Home in the Spring* (Walla Walla, Wash.: Pioneer Press, 1984), 276.

7. Lockley, *Conversations with Pioneer Women,* 6–11.

8. Schlissel et al., *Far from Home,* 22.

9. Ibid., 32.

10. Brown, *Gentle Tamers,* 49.

11. Lockley, *Conversations with Pioneer Women,* 383.

5. MIDWIVES

1. Brown, *Gentle Tamers,* 204.

2. Lydia M. Waters, "Account of a Trip Across the Plains in 1855," *Society of California Pioneers Quarterly* VI (1929), 64.

3. Lockley, *Conversations with Pioneer Women,* 283.

4. Bennett, *We'll All Go Home in the Spring,* 297.

5. Thompson, *Daughter of a Pioneer*, 39.

6. Patricia Preciado Martin, *Songs My Mother Sang to Me: An Oral History of Mexican American Women* (Tucson: University of Arizona Press, 1992), 107.

7. Thompson, *Daughter of a Pioneer*, 250.

8. Levy, *They Saw the Elephant*, 73.

9. Lockley, *Conversations with Pioneer Women*, 47.

10. Schlissel et al., *Far from Home*, 28.

11. Levy, *They Saw the Elephant*, 76.

12. Lockley, *Conversations with Pioneer Women*, 237.

13. Ibid., 293.

14. Ibid., 167–168.

15. Ibid., 266.

16. Ibid., 291.

17. Susan Evans McCloud, *Not in Vain* (Salt Lake City: Bookcraft, 1984), 138–140.

18. Levy, *They Saw the Elephant*, 76.

19. Lorraine Fletcher, "Nineteenth Century Midwife: Some Recollections," *Oregon Historical Quarterly* 70 (March 1969), 49.

6. NEIGHBORS

1. Levy, *They Saw the Elephant*, 194.

2. Ibid., 195.

3. Sara McAllister Hartman, Memoirs (expanded manuscript). University of Washington Libraries, Manuscripts and Archives Division, 2.

4. Lockley, *Conversations with Pioneer Women*, 221.

5. Ross, *Westward the Women*, 66.

6. Hartman, Memoirs, 5.

7. Bennett, *We'll All Go Home in the Spring*, 297.

8. Ross, *Westward the Women*, 21.

9. Martin, *Songs My Mother Sang to Me*, 56.

10. Thompson, *Daughter of a Pioneer*, 90.

11. Martin, *Songs My Mother Sang to Me*, 107.

12. Levy, *They Saw the Elephant*, 76.

13. *Tsagigla'lal.*

14. Martin, *Songs My Mother Sang to Me*, 56.

15. *Tsagigla'lal.*

7. WOMEN ON THEIR OWN

1. Lockley, *Conversations with Pioneer Women*, 165.

2. John H. Clark, "Overland to the Goldfields of California in 1852," *Kansas Historical Quarterly* XI, 1942, 236.

3. Lockley, *Conversations with Pioneer Women*, 64.

4. Louise Clappe (Dame Shirley), *The Shirley Letters: From the California Mines, 1851–1852*. Edited by Carl I. Wheat (New York: Knopf, 1961), 326.

5. Elizabeth D. S. Geer, "Diary," Oregon Pioneer Association Transactions XXXV (Portland, 1907), 173.

6. Bennett, *We'll All Go Home in the Spring*, 147.

7. Lockley, *Conversations with Pioneer Women*, 64–65.

8. Hartman, Memoirs, 4.

9. Esther Mumford, ed., *Seven Stars and Orion* (Seattle: Anansi Press, 1986), 130.

10. Luchetti and Olwell, *Women of the West*, 114.

11. Lockley, *Conversations with Pioneer Women*, 65.

12. Ross, *Westward the Women*, 171.

13. Lockley, *Conversations with Pioneer Women*, 168.

Material on pages 11, 14, 27, 36, 59, 60, 63, 64, and 70 is quoted from *They Saw the Elephant: Women in the California Gold Rush* © 1990 by JoAnn Levy (Camden. Conn.: Archon Books, 1990).

FURTHER READING

BOOKS

Aaseng, Nathan. *From Rags to Riches.* Minneapolis: Lerner, 1990.

Alter, Judith. *Growing Up in the Old West.* Chicago: Watts, 1991.

———. *Women of the Old West.* New York: Watts, 1989.

Bakeless, John, ed. *The Journals of Lewis and Clark.* New York: Penguin, 1964.

Bennett, Robert Allen. *We'll All Go Home in the Spring.* Walla Walla, Wash.: Pioneer Press, 1984.

Binns, Archie. *Peter Skene Ogden: Fur Trader.* Portland, Ore.: Binford and Mort, 1967.

Blumberg, Rhoda. *The Great American Gold Rush.* New York: Macmillan, 1989.

Brown, Dee. *Gentle Tamers: Women in the Old Wild West.* Lincoln: University of Nebraska Press, 1968.

———. *Hear That Lonesome Whistle Blow: Railroads in the West.* New York: Holt, 1977.

Carter, Harvey L. *Dear Old Kit.* Norman: University of Oklahoma Press, 1968.

Clappe, Louise (Dame Shirley). *The Shirley Letters: From the California Mines, 1850–1852.* Edited by Carl I. Wheat. New York: Knopf, 1961.

Clemens, Samuel Langhorne. *Roughing It.* New York: Holt, Rinehart and Winston, 1965.

De Nevi, Don, and Noel Moholy. *Junípero Serra.* New York: Harper and Row, 1985.

Erickson, Paul. *Daily Life in a Covered Wagon.* Washington, D.C.: Preservation Press, 1994.

Fischer, Christiane, ed. *Let Them Speak for Themselves: Women in the American West, 1849–1900.* Hamden, Conn.: Archon, 1977.

Fisher, Leonard Everett. *The Oregon Trail.* New York: Holiday, 1990.

Harte, Bret. *The Luck of Roaring Camp.* Providence, Rhode Island: Jamestown, 1976.

Hoobler, Dorothy, and Thomas Hoobler. *Treasure in the Stream: The Story of a Gold Rush Girl.* Morristown, New Jersey: Silver Burdett, 1991.

Jessett, Thomas E. *Chief Spokan Garry.* Minneapolis: T. S. Denison, 1960.

Johnson, Paul C., ed. *The California Missions.* Menlo Park, Cal.: Lane Book, 1964.

Katz, William. *The Black West.* Seattle: Open Hand, 1987.

Lapp, Rudolph. *Blacks in Gold Rush California.* New Haven: Yale University Press, 1977.

Lasky, Kathryn. *Beyond the Divide.* New York: Dell, 1986.

Levy, Jo Ann. *They Saw the Elephant.* Hamden, Conn.: Archon, 1990.

Lewis, Oscar. *Sutter's Fort: Gateway to the Gold Fields.* New York: Knopf, 1976.

Luchetti, Cathy, and Carol Olwell. *Women of the West.* Berkeley: Antelope Island Press, 1982.

McNeer, May. *The California Gold Rush*. New York: Random House, 1987.

Meltzer, Milton. *The Chinese Americans: A History in Their Own Words*. New York: HarperCollins, 1980.

Morris, Juddi. *The Harvey Girls: The Women Who Civilized the West*. New York: Walker, 1994.

Moynihan, Ruth B., Susan Armitage, and Christiane Fischer Duchamp, eds. *So Much to Be Done: Women Settlers on the Mining and Ranching Frontier*. Lincoln: University of Nebraska Press, 1990.

Nabakov, Peter. *Native American Testimony: An Anthology of Indian and White Relations, First Encounter to Dispossession*. New York: HarperCollins, 1972.

Rappaport, Doreen, ed. *American Women: Their Lives in Their Words*. New York: HarperCollins, 1992.

Ray, Delia. *Gold, the Klondike Adventure*. New York: Lodestar, 1989.

Schlissel, Lillian. *Women's Diaries of the Westward Journey*. New York: Shocken, 1982.

Smith, Carter. *Bridging the Continent: A Sourcebook on the American West*. Brookfield, Conn.: Millbrook Press, 1992.

Steber, Rick. *Grandpa's Stories*. Prineville, Ore.: Bonanza, 1991.

Stewart, George R. *The Pioneers Go West*. New York: Random House, 1987.

Stratton, Joanna. *Pioneer Women*. New York: Simon and Schuster, 1982.

The Trailblazers. *The Old West*. New York: Time-Life Books, 1979.

Tunis, Edwin. *Frontier Living*. New York: HarperCollins, 1976.

Van Steenwyk, Elizabeth. *The California Gold Rush: West with the Forty-niners.* Chicago: Watts, 1991.

Watt, James W. *Journal of Mule Train Packing in Eastern Washington in the 1860s.* Fairfield, Wash.: Ye Galleon Press, 1978.

Weis, Norman D. *Helldorados, Ghosts and Camps of the Old Southwest.* Caldwell, Idaho: Caxton Printers, 1977.

Wilder, Laura Ingalls. *West from Home.* New York: HarperCollins, 1974.

Wilson, Elinor. *Jim Beckwourth: Black Mountain Man and War Chief of the Crows.* Norman: University of Oklahoma Press, 1972.

Young, Alida O. *Land of the Iron Dragon.* New York: Doubleday, 1978.

TAPES AND COMPUTER SOFTWARE

American West: Myth and Reality, Clear View, CD-ROM.

Dare, Bluff, or Die, Software Tool Works, CD-ROM, DOS.

Miner's Cave, MECC, Apple II.

Morrow, Honere. *On to Oregon!* Recorded Books, Inc., Prince Frederick, Md. Three cassettes.

Murphy's Minerals, MECC, Apple II.

Oregon Trail II, CD-ROM, Windows.

The Oregon Trail, MECC, Apple II, MS-DOS, 1990.

Santa Fe Trail (Educational Activities).

Steber, Rick. *Grandpa's Stories.* Bonanza. Cassette.

Wagons West, Focus Media, 485 South Broadway, Suite 12, Hicksville, New York, 11801.

INDEX

Anthony, Susan B., 81

Barnes, Jane, 26, 32, 33
Biles, Rachel Malick, 14, 51, 52, 53, 54, 60
black women, 36–37
brides
  advice for, 59, 68–69
  army, 54
  arranged marriages, 42
  courtship, 20, 49
  desperate reasons, marrying for, 52, 79
  donation land claim, 36
  loneliness, 15, 65, 71
  mail-order brides, 37–38
  marriage, 48–49, 51–52
  marriages of convenience, 33, 35
  "Mercer Girls," 39–42
  Native American, 11, 14, 18, 21, 33
  "picture brides," 42–46
  young, 49

cattle, dangers from, 61–62
childbirth, 54, 55, 57–59, 60, 63, 72
  celebrations, 60
  death during, 54, 59
  doctors at, 55, 63
  midwives, role of, 57–59
Chinese immigrants, 29, 30
cholera, 72–74
civilizing effect of women, 13, 36
Columbia River, 21, 49

"daughters of joy," 29

death
accidents, from, 61–62, 72
childbirth, during, 54, 59, 72
children, among, 59–60, 72
diseases, from, 59
doctors, 55, 63, 81
Donation Land Claim Act, 35, 75

families
death's effect on, 74
large, 61
young women traveling West with, 14, 49
Farnham, Eliza, 36
Fort Astoria, 21, 23

gold rush, 14, 59, 78

half-breeds (métis), 24
hardships faced by settlers, 61, 66, 67, 71
hurdy-gurdy girls, 32

immigrants, 29, 30, 46, 59
finding brides for, 42–44
importing women, 27, 29, 30, 38–41
independent women, 14, 69, 80, 81

Japanese immigrants, 30, 42–44, 46, 59

land claims, 35, 36, 75, 76

McLoughlin, John, 22, 24, 35, 65
medical care, 57, 59, 62. See also midwives; nurses and nursing.
Mercer, Asa Shinn, 38–42
midwives
breast feeding, 60
husbands as, 59
remedies, 57, 58, 69
special skills of, 57, 69
missionaries, 33, 35, 80

Native Americans, 17, 65, 66
women, 17–19, 21, 22
nurses and nursing, 58, 78

Owens-Adair, Bethenia, 67, 80

Paiute Indians, 19, 20
prostitutes, 27, 30

reasons for women to go West, 14, 26–27, 33
relatives, 18, 23, 43, 64
rights for women, 81

Rivet, Julia, 17, 21
Roberts, Nancy Ann, 58

Sacagawea, 17
self-sufficiency of women,
    70, 77
Shipp, Ellis Reynolds, 62,
    63, 81
shortage of women, 11, 14,
    36, 38, 49
slavery, women in, 29, 80
Spalding, Eliza, 26, 35
"squaw men," 22
survival, 54, 67, 74

tanka poetry, 46, 71
Tomita, Teiko Matsui, 46, 71
Townsend, Susanna, 60, 63

voting rights, 81

wagon trains, 48, 55, 62, 72,
    74
Walker, Mary Richardson,
    33–35, 60, 66, 81

Washington, Mary Jane
    Cooness, 70
Whitman, Narcissa Prentiss,
    11, 26, 33, 35, 64, 80, 81
widows
    Civil War, 38
    decisions to be made by,
        73–74
    determination to survive,
        74–75
    good health, importance
        of, 75
    living on the land, 75, 78
    loneliness of, 79
    "Mercer Girls," coming
        West with, 39, 41
    remarriage, 78–79
    work for, 76–78
Willamette Valley, 49
Women's Medical College
    of Philadelphia, 63, 81
work, 12, 15, 38, 44–46
    going West to find, 14
    types of work for women,
        76–77, 78, 81